FAMILY FIRST

Deshawn's Big Race

Monica Allen

Family First: Deshawn's Big Race
Copyright © 2021 Monica Allen

ISBN: 979-8-9851668-0-4 (paperback)
ISBN: 979-8-9851668-1-1 (ebook)

Dedication

I want to thank my Savior for being a comfort and the ultimate guide. My loving family for allowing me the space to create in my own way. To my mom, Jennette, for her unconditional love and support, my five children, Mya, Mikayla, Kacey Jr., Malia and Kyle, for being my inspiration, my husband, Kacey, for being my biggest cheerleader. My Vault girls for their support and encouragement. My Best friends, Summer, Lateefah and Heather, for total unwavering support. And all the children I have had the opportunity to meet and interact with over the years. This book is dedicated to all of you!

On an early summer morning, the sun peeked through the bedroom window as the curtains swayed back and forth from the wind of the ceiling fan.

Mika and Deshawn were fast asleep.

Dad walked in. "Good morning! Time to rise and shine!" he called.

Deshawn opened one eye and gave a sleepy smile.

Then Mama walked in, singing, "Wake up, sleepyheads!"

Her voice woke Mika, who sat up and reached high for her morning stretch.

"Why are you waking us so early?" Deshawn asked, rubbing his eyes. Suddenly, it hit him. "Wait! Today is our family trip!"

Mika and Deshawn both jumped out of bed. Deshawn began to stuff his favorite games into his bag. He really tried to concentrate on packing, but he was distracted. His mind was too focused on other things.

Mika packed some of her favorite things as well. Deshawn looked over at what she was bringing and shook his head.

"Makeup?" Deshawn said, rolling his eyes. "We're going to the lake house to swim, fish, and play games. Why do you need makeup?"

Mika tried to act as if she didn't hear her brother. "I wonder if Semaj will win the lake race again this year," she said with a smirk.

Deshawn's teasing smile turned into a frown.

Last year, Deshawn had narrowly lost the race to his older cousin, Semaj, and it had been on his mind ever since. He didn't want to talk about the race with Mika. He didn't want to talk about it with anyone. All he wanted to do was win.

"Whatever! Pack your stupid makeup." Deshawn zipped up his bag and left in a huff. He headed out to the garage to get in one final workout before they left. He did twenty-five push-ups, one hundred sit-ups, and twenty pull-ups, then finished by flexing in the mirror to see his results.

He looked as strong as he felt. He was ready.

...At least he hoped he was.

After a quick breakfast, they were ready to get on the road for the long drive.

Mama enjoyed the changing scenery, and Dad spotted the big birds soaring above. Mika and Deshawn played games and watched videos on their phones.

Halfway to the lake house, they spotted their favorite truck stop. "Can we…" Mika began to ask, but Dad was way ahead of her. He was already on the offramp. They piled back into the car ten minutes later with souvenirs and junk food.

When they finally arrived at the cabin eight hours later, Mama and Dad unloaded the bags while Mika and Deshawn ran out of the car in opposite directions. Mika headed inside. Deshawn jogged down to the lake, hoping that seeing it would calm his nerves.

Deshawn heard the sound of tires rolling on gravel behind him. He rushed up to the back of the cabin to see his older cousin Semaj get out of his family's car. Suddenly, Deshawn felt nervous again. He wasn't ready to face his cousin, so he snuck inside through the back.

Semaj, his sister Jennifer, and his brother Kaleb, walked into the kitchen where Mika was setting up a makeover session. The moment they saw the makeup, Semaj and Kaleb turned right around and headed to the game room.

In the hallway, Semaj saw Deshawn going upstairs. "Hey, Deshawn," he called. "I'm ready to win the lake race again!"

Deshawn didn't know what came over him. Without thinking, he opened his mouth and answered with a challenge of his own. "Why wait? Let's go now!"

As soon as the words left his mouth, he panicked. He couldn't believe he had uttered those words, but he couldn't take them back now.

"Unless you're not ready," he doubled down with a smirk, trying to match Semaj's confidence.

"You wish!" Semaj said laughing. "Let's do it!"

All the cousins came running when they saw Deshawn and Semaj headed to the lake. They had been waiting for this challenge all year.

As Deshawn stepped onto the beach, he forced himself to stop for a moment. He took a deep breath to relax his racing heart.

Semaj looked calm. He was swinging his arms like a professional swimmer. Deshawn ignored his cousin's confidence and tried to focus on winning.

At the edge of the lake, they lined up, ready to go. Mika pulled a bandana from her hair and held it up. She watched her brother nervously.

"On your mark, get set, go!" she called, lowering her hand to start the race.

Semaj and Deshawn ran into the water, splashing loudly until they were waist deep, then began to swim. The cousins chanted and shouted, running along the water's rim and cheering them on. But soon the voices faded, and all Deshawn heard was his heart beating and the light splash of water.

Semaj's strokes seemed to slice through the water easily. He swam as if the race wasn't a challenge. He even turned over and did a few backstrokes so he could wave to the cheering crowd on the shore!

Meanwhile, Deshawn kept swimming steadily. He could see the finish line, the dock, not too far off.

Deshawn was so close—he could almost touch the dock! He might actually win!

Suddenly, in the water behind him, Deshawn heard frantic splashing and a loud cry for help. Deshawn turned his head quickly to see Semaj thrashing in the water.

Deshawn immediately went into action, pushing off the post at the dock's edge and speeding through the water with all the grace and ease of a dolphin.

"What's wrong?" he called to his cousin.

"Cramp!" Semaj replied in a painful voice. "Hurry!"

When Deshawn reached Semaj, he put his arm across his cousin's chest and began to swim slowly, kicking his legs and reaching out his free arm with big strokes.

"I got you, Semaj," he said gently. "You're going to be fine."

By the time they reached the dock, the others were already there. They all worked together to pull Semaj out of the water. Kaleb ran over to check on his brother's leg, and Jennifer spread out a towel so he could lay down. Mika ran over to Deshawn and hugged him tight.

"Are you okay?" Mika asked.

"Yeah, I'm fine. Just wiped out!" Deshawn replied, struggling to find his breath.

"I'm so proud of you," Mika said. "Not only did you save Semaj, but you also won the race!"

Deshawn was confused. "What?" he asked, still breathing heavily.

"YOU WON THE RACE!" Mika shouted happily. Deshawn looked puzzled. Mika laughed. "I can't believe you didn't realize it. You got over to Semaj so quickly by kicking off the dock. That means you touched the finish line first, which makes you the winner!"

Deshawn remembered doing so, but oddly still had a hard time believing it. He was just still very tired.

Deshawn took a deep breath and let out a sigh. He then looked over at Semaj and asked, "You okay, Cousin?"

Semaj nodded. "I am now, thanks to you!"

Mika and Deshawn helped Semaj stand up. They walked back to the cabin together slowly, to give both boys a chance to catch their breath.

As they walked, Semaj reached out to Deshawn for a fist bump. "Thanks for the help. I didn't know you could swim so fast. Nice job out there," he said with a sheepish smile.

Deshawn and Mika both grinned. Deshawn did his best to hide his excitement.

"Thanks, cuz. I appreciate that."

The kids could smell the food as they approached the cabin.

"You all must've followed your noses. Dinner is ready!" Dad said happily.

"That's great news, because we're extra hungry!" Semaj said, putting his arm around Deshawn.

They played games, ate, laughed, and each recounted their versions of the race so many times that their parents felt like they had been there to witness it for themselves.

The late afternoon turned to evening as the sun set. Fireflies danced lazily over the grass as the cousins lay on their backs together, looking up at the stars.

"The week always goes by so fast," Mika said wistfully. "I wish we had more time."

Jennifer laughed at her younger cousin. "We just arrived! We have a whole week of fun and games ahead of us."

"I wish it would last forever."

"Me too," Deshawn said.

"Me three!" said Semaj with a laugh. "But now I have a whole year to train before our next race."

"I look forward to it," Deshawn said, his wide grin hidden under the dark cover of night.

That night, snuggled in their beds, all the cousins fell asleep quickly—as they always did after a full day at the lake.

They were already planning the next trip in their dreams.

The End

Made in the USA
Middletown, DE
06 June 2022

66764669R00020